Published by Tate Publishing & Enterprises, LLC
127 E. Trade Center Terrace | Mustang, Oklahoma 73064 USA
1.888.361.9473 | www.tatepublishing.com

Tate Publishing is committed to excellence in the publishing industry. The company reflects the philosophy established by the founders, based on Psalm 68:11,
"The Lord gave the word and great was the company of those who published it."

Book design copyright © 2015 by Tate Publishing, LLC. All rights reserved.
Cover and interior design by Rhezette Fiel
Illustrations by Louise charm Pulvera

Published in the United States of America

ISBN: 978-1-63367-353-3
Juvenile Fiction / Animals / General
14.11.25

For my daughter, Rebecca

Love,

Daddy.

Good morning, love! Rise and shine.
How did you sleep?
Do you remember what we
are going to do today?

~~ ❀ ~~

That's right! We are going to the zoo.
What animals do you think we will see
first at the zoo?

Look! There are the tigers and lions.
They are so quiet and strong.

Oh, now here are the bears,
all fuzzy and warm.

You like the silly monkeys, don't you, love? They are so funny!

~~ ✿ ~~

I love the birds with all those beautiful
colors. Their songs are soft like clouds
and sweet as honey.

Wow! That must be the tall giraffe.
I wonder how they drink
with such long necks.

What would you do if you lived under the sea like the fish? I think I might explore a deep cave or an old shipwreck!

Hmm, I'm getting hungry. How about you? Yum, apples are my favorite part of lunch.

Now, snow cones for dessert. What a perfect little treat.

Snow, that reminds me!

We almost forgot about the proud
penguins. Burr, they look really cold.

Last but not least, the enormous
elephant that moves like molasses.

Well, well it looks like the elephant is not the only one who is moving slow.

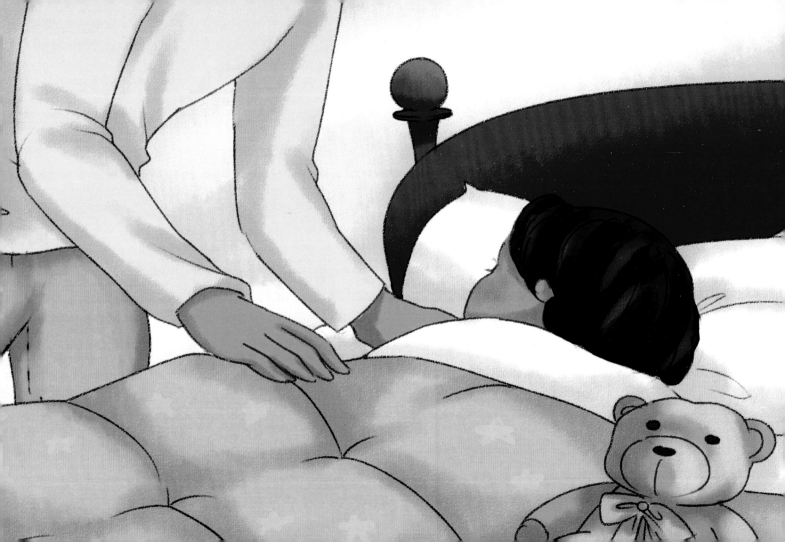

What a wonderful day.
Thank you for sharing it with me.
I will remember this day
as long as I live!

Good night. Sleep tight.
Never forget that you are loved.

e|LIVE

listen|imagine|view|experience

AUDIO BOOK DOWNLOAD INCLUDED WITH THIS BOOK!

In your hands you hold a complete digital entertainment package. In addition to the paper version, you receive a free download of the audio version of this book. Simply use the code listed below when visiting our website. Once downloaded to your computer, you can listen to the book through your computer's speakers, burn it to an audio CD or save the file to your portable music device (such as Apple's popular iPod) and listen on the go!

How to get your free audio book digital download:

1. Visit www.tatepublishing.com and click on the e|LIVE logo on the home page.
2. Enter the following coupon code:
   c8c9-1941-c44e-e273-af84-ef09-2c01-a0b1
3. Download the audio book from your e|LIVE digital locker and begin enjoying your new digital entertainment package today!